Roderick Flanagan

Australian and other Poems

Roderick Flanagan

Australian and other Poems

ISBN/EAN: 9783337313715

Printed in Europe, USA, Canada, Australia, Japan

Cover: Foto ©Andreas Hilbeck / pixelio.de

More available books at **www.hansebooks.com**

AUSTRALIAN AND OTHER POEMS.

AUSTRALIAN

AND OTHER

POEMS

BY

RODERICK J. FLANAGAN

SYDNEY

EDWARD F. FLANAGAN, 586 GEORGE STREET.

DUBLIN: M. H. GILL AND SON

1887

M. H. GILL AND SON, PRINTERS, DUBLIN.

PREFACE.

THE author of the following poems died twenty-five years ago. Some of them appeared in various Sydney newspapers, while he was yet living, but many are now printed for the first time. Such exercises were rather the solace and diversion than the serious business of any portion of his literary career—a career which was, unfortunately, as brief as it was full of promise. Distinguished among the journalists of his day, he also made no unimportant mark in what may be termed the regular field of letters. His work on New South Wales, the publication of which, in London, was coincident with his death in that city, at the early age of thirty-three, is justly regarded as a permanently valuable contribution to Australian history. Besides this, he wrote a series of papers in the *Empire* news-

paper on the Aborigines of Australia, which
were considered to have shed much light on
the manners and customs of that now almost
extinct race. It is to be regretted that his
death prevented the publication of those
essays in book form.

Much that passes for brilliant poetry now-
a-days is generally a matter of patience and
labour, combined with verbal dexterity and
what may be described as a skilful process
of assimilation. The faculty alluded to may
exist unmingled with a single particle of the
genuine quality which it counterfeits. It was
decidedly otherwise in Mr. Flanagan's case.
That he possessed at least the poetic tempera-
ment in a strong degree there can be no
doubt. Had he assiduously cultivated the gift
he might possibly have struck a memorable
note. As it is, there is in these fugitive pro-
ductions not a little, perhaps, which even the
most coldly critical reader can hardly fail to
admire : a play of fancy which is occasionally

very graceful ; energetic and picturesque description ; and, above all, a strain of feeling which is unaffectedly simple, generous, and manly.

For such readers, however, the volume is not intended, but chiefly for those to whom it will be a memorial of a friend whose kindly heart was not less calculated to inspire affection than his abilities were to command respect.

November, 1886.

CONTENTS.

———◆———

CONTENTS.

CONTENTS.

Australian and Other Poems.

—◦—◦—◦—

A SONG OF AUSTRALIA.

JANUARY 26, 1788.

Joy fills to-day my bosom, and it flies through every
    vein,
It comes as on the parchèd plain descends mid-
    summer rain ;
It fills my soul with gladness, e'en to aerial beings
    new,
As sunbeams fall on budding flowers when morning
    gilds the dew.

No more I'm like a maiden that's neglected in her
    bloom,
Doomed when bridals throng the highway to pine
    in lonely gloom ;

No more I'm like a blooming bride, who waits, 'mid
bright array,
For the coming of the bridegroom, whom Death
struck on the way.

No more I'm like a matron lone, whose husband and
whose sons
Lie slain where through the battle-throng the rude
Destroyer runs.
To-day bold suitors come in crowds, to-day I'm
wooed and won,
To-day the long-expected ones have found their
gladdened home.

To-day the founders of a race shall fill my broad
domains,
Shall wake the silence of my woods, shall swarm upon
my plains.
Have come, and shall not welcome meet, and shall
not guerdon high
Good greeting to their advent give, repay each toil-
wrung sigh ?

Fair are Britannia's fertile vales, with happy hamlets
    strown,
And fair are Gallia's hills and plains, for teeming
    vineyards known ;
The Arno flows through smiling lands where peasants
    know but glee ;
And stars that shine o'er Egypt's flood, earth's
    favoured regions see.

But not less rich than Britain's isles, and not less fair
    than France
Shall be the plains where, aftertime, my sons will lead
    the dance ;
And not more pure th' Italian skies than skies above
    my soil,
And streams as broad, as rich as Nile shall bless my
    peasants' toil.

Rich are the gifts Columbia gives to those who cross
    the wave,
Bright are the ores she brings to light, where delves
    the weary slave ;

But far more rich the gold I'll give, to glad my
vent'rous sons;
And, oh! to win its lustrous glance no tear of sad
slave runs!

Oh! to-day a joy unwonted within my heart holds
sway,
Such joy as feel the shipwrecked host, at sight of
coming day,
Such joy as feel the city's tribes, long pent by war's
alarms,
When, breathing in sweet fields again, they fly to
Freedom's arms.

THE DROWNED HAMLET.

Up from his orient star-gemmed couch the sun,
    revived, arose,
And as beseemed a guardian true, his searching
    glance he throws
On all those scenes that court his care—stream,
    woodland, hill, and plain,
The first at morn to fix his look, the last at daylight's
    wane.

As lighted up his glowing face, his glance more
    warmly fell
Adown that scene where, scanning close, he saw
    that all was well ;
And when at eve his parting rays give place to
    glimmering stars,
No sign he marks to dull his eye, no shade his glad-
    ness mars.

For all the land was deftly clad in sparkling June's
　　array—
Australia's June, where spring's mild reign usurps
　　warm summer's sway—
Bright blossoms thickly strewed the plain, the birds
　　made gayest show,
The herbage filled luxuriant fields—men said they
　　saw it grow.

And Gundagai! that twilight on no fairer scene did
　　close;
Joyous to view thy rustic bliss the Murrumbidgee
　　rose.
Careering past, his gallant flood, swelling, he seemed
　　to say :—
" No fairer scene on all my banks gladdened my
　　course to-day."

The twilight fast has darkened down into the gloom
　　of night;
Through every vine-clad lattice gleams the taper's
　　cheering light:

To seek relief from trivial cares the toilers forth
    repair,
The children round the matron group, to breathe the
    evening prayer.

The hour when Slumber claims her sway descends
    upon the scene,
Late-sitting guests, with gossip worn, are tending
    homewards seen,
No change, to note, the vale comes o'er, no fear the
    homes among,
The river, in his olden path, unswerving glides
    along.

The crescent night draws to its noon—amaze all
    hearts has thrilled;
The waters, rising, flood the floors—the town with
    cries is filled.
The mother, moaning, seeks her babes, whose limbs
    the waters lave,
The father plies his anxious skill to ward th' intruding
    wave.

Through all the night the danger grows, and when
    the morning beamed
How altered was the scene whereon the azure twilight
    streamed ;
It seemed as though the Bow of Hope had lost its
    promised sway,
And that the earth, with all its tribes, its sins again
    should pay.

The sun arose, as erst he came, but not as erst the
    scene
Whereon his cheering rays descend. Instead of
    landscape green
A wide extending waste of wave gave back his light-
    some glance,
Where 'mid the perches of the birds the reckless
    eddies dance.

And clust'ring on each roof-top, spared to yield such
    sad relief,
Were seen the hamlet's household, fast thralled in
    spell of grief ;

And in the trees were clinging some, with strength
    which faded fast,
And others, they had ceased to cling—their days were
    of the past.

A boat has left the desert shore, and see its oarsmen
    strong,
Against the rushing wreck and wave, make battle well
    and long.
That fragile bark, returning oft, receives the fainting
    host
Who 'scaped the flood, where haply all their best
    beloved were lost.

Give honour to those gallant men who fall in free-
    dom's cause,
And to those men their meed of praise who war
    'gainst wrongful laws;
But while all they who serve the weal requiting
    guerdons find,
Shall not the fate of those we sing full well be borne
    in mind?

They left the banks of Thames and Tweed and Erna's
    fern-rimmed mere,
And passed half earth's untraversed zone, new shrines
    and homes to rear;
They fought the fight of sternest life, with steady
    heart and hand,
And left their fate to landmark an unmonumented
    land.

When deep and rapid comes the flood by hamlets free
    from fear,
And when the rivers' lessening banks speak an
    abundant year,
Then, then shall Memory summon up the kindly tear
    and sigh,
For those whose fate has saddened o'er the name of
    Gundagai.

THE VALE OF MANLY.

SWEET Vale of Manly! when the eye first lights
With fire more pure, beholding all thy charms—
And when the murmuring lips, compelled, proclaim
In words inaudible, but most intense,
Thy hundred beauties; when with lingering gaze
Enchanted vision rests on every scene
By fav'ring Nature formed on plan for thee
And only thee, with skill unequalled wrought;
How many musings all with grace suffused,
Proportioned to the view, crowd on the mind!
The gently-sloping plain whereon—like robe
Of green, with mimic blossoms strewn—close set
The foliage and the flowers commingle;
The unobtrusive stream that courts the shade
Suggestive of the chain of pearl that finds
'Mid golden curls a nest wherefrom it peeps
With timid glance, as fearful lest it lose
Its pleasant home; these and unnumbered charms
Beside, in sep'rate order rise to hold,
Like bird in beauty's bower, the Fancy caged.

Upon the swelling, noisy waves intent,
That with a blustering and an awkward grace
Pay court where ocean comes to steal a glance,
I pictured thee a maiden fair, hard-wooed
By lover grey—a gallant poor in years,
But rich in gold and silver; ships that bear
From every clime their proper fruits and wares;
Spreading domains and stately mansions stored
With all the wealth of art. In the loud roar
The waves sent forth, methought I heard the tale
The lover told to win the blushing fair.
He spoke of bridal train that rich in robes,
Nor less in heartfelt joy, should lead the way,
When to the altar the bright concourse went,
By prancing steeds and glittering chariots borne.
He spoke of waiting train, of pomp, of show,
Of the high festival that frequent comes
Whereof his bride is queen ; and when his speech,
That wearied by its length and haughty sound,
Was done, the pompous lover vainly tried
To smile, and puffed his rosy cheeks that glowed
With tinge imparted by the viny juice.

Anon I gazed upon the placid bay,
That murmuring laves the circling beach that lies

In silent, sheltered solitude within,
Where the capes, closing towards the ocean swell,
Protect the lustrous harbour from the blast,
The surge, and the too frequent haze, and then
Methought I saw the same fair maiden wooed
By youthful lover, nestling at her knees.
In submiss tones, but suasive, he did speak
Of cottage home in well-cared garden set
'Mid circling trees that teem with tropic fruits;
Of walks beneath eve's azure canopy,
When silence sits amid the golden stars:
Of mutual love that grows as years decay;
Of sweet retirement from the frowns and sneers
The vulgar and the very-wise put on ;
Of youth in modest happiness enjoyed ;
Of age all peace, and death like to a sleep.

Disturbed with thoughts conflicting, still the maid
Blushes and droops her eyes, that yet reveal
In growing lustre that she scorns not love.
Not cruel formed, to neither will she speak
The harsh denial. Though her kindest glance
Rests on the youth, to neither speaks she aye ;

But adds to their already ardent love
By each fresh charm her doubting calls to life.

So Vale of Manly! wooed by Ocean wild
That pours in homage at thy feet his waves,
And by the gentle Spirit of the Bay,
That brings the sylvan graces in his train,
To spend their skill in decking out thy bowers,
To neither dost thou yield thy blooming charms,
But well dost deem that in the privilege
Of wooing, all their love is well repaid

BONDI STANZAS.

WRITTEN ON A VISIT TO BONDI BEACH, AFTER AN
ABSENCE OF SOME YEARS.*

SWEET Bondi of the surging waves,
   The snowy sands and twinkling shells !
Again I greet the sea that laves
   Thy sunny beach, thy coral dells !

How often, in my boyhood's day,
   When Fancy soar'd on new-fledg'd wing,
I've lov'd to list the sounding lay
   Thy rolling waves incessant sing !

---

* Bondi Beach is situate about five miles south of the Sydney
Heads, and on a line, in an easterly direction, with the City of
Sydney. It is a mile in extent, and over its entire length the
waves of the Pacific roll continually in mountainous swells. The
tumultuous roar of the waters on the beach, and among the
neighbouring rocks, is at all times considerable, and during
certain phases of the atmosphere is distinctly heard throughout
the eastern quarters of the city, at a distance of six or seven
miles.

How often with my joyous shout,
   Thy shelt'ring rocks have loudly rung,
When sporting free, 'mid truant rout,
   I gamboll'd thy wild scenes among!

And still, unchang'd, thy charms I feel;
   And still I gaze but to admire!
Not years can make those charms unreal,
   Nor ages fade thy bright attire!

No ancient tale, no classic lore,
   Amid thy scenes like spirits bide;
Nor to thy vales, as spots of fame,
   Does history point in glowing pride!

No moss-grown pile, no mystic tower,
   Attractive rise to spell-bound ken;
No shrine of druid, king, or saint,
   Inspires the pencil or the pen.

Nor do thy heights, approving, smile
   O'er fields by martyr'd heroes trod,
Such as at Marathon, erewhile,
   Crush'd Persia's hosts, and broke her rod.

But what though Fame her charms deny
  While Fancy yields such precious store!
What, though thy past be starless sky!
  Thy future's sun will glow the more.

Here, standing 'mid thy girding wood,
  I see yon city's limits bound—
As Rome of old her Tiber's flood—
  Those mirror'd bays now circling round.

And, gazing landward from the sea,
  The wild is chang'd, the desert gone,
And vine-clad hill and fruitful lea
  Are vocal with the rustic song.

Again I turn to greet the wave,
  And ships unnumber'd stand array'd
And men are there as strong and brave
  As ever flush'd in war or trade.

And, fairest sight! o'er land and main
  Waves Freedom's banner uncontroll'd,
And Freedom, chief of heav'nly train,
  E'er bounteous, squanders bliss untold.

3

And Peace, descending, quits the skies,
　　And Science plies her wondrous hand,
And Art her magic skill supplies
　　To spread abundance o'er the land.

This, this, sweet Bondi! surging shore!
　　The alter'd scene shall list thy lay,
When fleeting ages pile their store
　　Of greatness, gath'ring day by day.

AUSTRALIAN WINTER.

CHILL is the season, yet so bright the rays
  The sun diffuses from his northern home,
That, like a well-proved friend who distant strays
  His spell beneficent is slow to roam.

The woods are bright, although their sheen grows
    less,
  Like bride who lays her wedding-garb aside;
The waters sparkle, though in mellowness,
  Like beauty's smile when youth has veiled its pride.

The hoar-frost marks the grassy lawn at morn,
  But fades when the first matin beam appears,
Till earth grows bright, as those erewhile forlorn,
  Joy when their hope a sunlit aspect wears.

We miss the leafless wood, the frost-bound earth,
  The waters sealed within their icy bed:
We miss the snow that folds the autumn's birth,
  Like shrouds that lie around the early dead.

We miss the robin twittering on the sill,
    Shut from the hedge that late was all his own,
The frugal snipe that sips the freezeless rill,
    The thrifty sparrow, and the blackbird lone.

Vain too we seek the social charms that live
    Around the thronging hearth, and well-piled board,
When winter's terrors doubled value give
    To all the wealth domestic virtues hoard.

Bright change to Spring's delightful bloom we
        want—
    Our fadeless woods know neither spring nor fall;
We miss the visions that the soul enchant,
    When Hope depicts the teeming year's recall.

Thus though the clime from rigours may be free,
    It wants what rougher zones are glad to boast;
Thus may we learn that by the wise decree,
    All have some proper bliss, the neediest most.

LINES, SUGGESTED BY A HAWTHORN IN THE BOTANIC GARDENS, SYDNEY.

As some brave soldier who has lost
His youth and strength 'mid battle tost,
Finds him, when age displays its frost,
     A castaway.
From home and kindred's kindly cheer
By doom or chance an exile drear;
Even such, old tree, the fate you bear,
     A sylvan stray.

Thy shrivelled stem, thy puny fruit,
The aspect of thy leafy suit,
Tell in this soil thy pining root
     Finds not its home.
While Fancy hears thy leaves among,
The tale where memories are sung,
Of the old lands wherefrom you sprung,
     Far o'er the foam.

Listing that tale, what visions rise !
A group of children meets our eyes,
With joyous looks and mirthful cries,
        That glad the swains.
And one is chosen Queen of May ;
Her golden ringlets wildly stray
Beneath a crown of blossoms gay,
        And daisy chains.

Next comes a youth whose idle gait,
Full well proclaims his truant state ;
Or, if he works, 'tis not to sate
        Dull learning's greed.
With earnest face and piercing eyes,
He cons each bush for birds'-nest prize ;
Or, climbing, from the bramble tries
        Its fruit to lead.

Beside the thorn a young man stands,
When home have sped the toiling bands
And evening's veil gives all the lands
        A grateful shade ;

His eyes rest on the farm-house near,
For one is there than life more dear;
The casement moves—she'll soon be here,
      His darling maid.

'Tis winter, and the hedge is bleak
What leads that group such shade to seek
Their home stood where ascends the reek
      In yonder vale.
The mother's tears are silent shed,
Above her children's roofless bed
The father strides with measured tread,
      Where frets the gale.

A chariot moves in stately show,
There, near the highway, hedges grow,
The peasants, as they pass, bend low,
      To him sits there.
Behind a thorn a flash is seen,
The air resounds a musket's din;
A corse that chariot within,
      Finds gory bier.

Thus not in vain, transplanted tree.
Thy venerated form we see
Where sylvan rarities agree,
     In order bright.
A poet, story-teller, seer,
Among the trees, you fill their sphere
With lore, tradition, and, more dear,
     Romance's light.

MEMORIES OF HOME.

Down in the solitude of thought, where hopes well-
 garnered dwell,
Where treasured up, our richer store lies safely kept
 and well,
There meting out the brilliant rays, which from
 their lustre come,
Lie safe-embowered, like ocean's pearls, these memories of home.

In varied shape these mem'ries flock, their fav'rite
 guise come list:
They're tending sprites which hover round, like
 seraphs in a mist
Of light evolved from spirit-land, and ever point
 away
To where our earlier joys had birth, our earliest longings stay.

They point to where the daisied field and fragrant
    plain extend,
Where silv'ry brooks, 'mid verdant meads, their
    bubbling passage wend,
Where the lark, at morning startled, when the
    shadows tend to west,
Soars, bearing up her matin hymn, then carols o'er
    her nest.

Where the reaper blithely whistles, while falls the
    teeming grain,
Where the maid, some love tale warbling, responds
    in rustic strain,
While laughing children, angel-eyed, with cheeks of
    blooming hue,
Fill groves surrounding with their song, there oftimes
    point they too.

And now to scenes more solemn do they call the
    vision back,
As where in old historic lands, grey age has left his
    track ;

The blood-dew'd fields, in story famed, come up before our gaze,
And heroes and heroic deeds, long sank in time's
deep haze.

Comes rising up each well-marked spot, by grey-
beard peasants shown,
Where Wrong awhile in arms prevail'd, perhaps where
Freedom won ;
Where erst some patriot chieftain called his willing
clansmen round,
And rushed to battle with his hosts where foemen
strewed the ground.

And wide-streamed rivers, in whose floods reflected
we behold
The homes and bowers of kings and bards who lived
in days of old,
Pass by in solemn, grand array, and as we gaze we
think
How many ages men have toiled, fought, loved,
beside their brink !

And ruins bleak, and temples old, by time or age
　　o'erthrown,
Rise up to mark where tomb-stones lie, by fun'ral
　　weeds o'ergrown,
While struggle with their darksome shade the antique
　　lines which show
The names and stories of the dust which mould'ring
　　lies below.

And lakes with breast of azure tinge and reedy zones
　　appear,
Where, 'mid surrounding meadow-lands, we whiled
　　the vernal year,
And lowing herd and bleating flocks live in our
　　fancy's eye,
As when in life's bright morning-time, these visions
　　passed us by.

Where'er a touch of Nature's hand has struck one
　　early string,
There chiefly tend those airy sprites on gay and
　　lightsome wing.

Where'er a brilliant joy has gleamed, a cherished
    hope lies hid
There go and come this wakeful band, untutored and
    unbid.

And often in joy's winter time, when cheerless
    bodings press,
When th' exile deems himself alone, or feels his
    hopes grow less,
This wizard band will flock around, and with one
    magic stroke
Call visions up, the brightest far on which thought
    e'er awoke.

All pleasures in the future dream'd by prophets or by
    seers,
They'll realise in charms which lie in dreams of by-
    gone years,
With more than song's excelling art, a blissful calm
    they'll find,
And driving hence each growing fear, they'll leave
    repose behind.

Then, whether in your gladsome hour or in your
    drooping mood,
Welcome and cherish when they come this aerial
    sisterhood;
In all the ways of life they'll be a solace by your
    side,
And while they make you better men, they'll form
    your safest guide.

LINES,

WHEN from the shore the waving hand
   Gives mute but eloquent good-bye,
What heart so cold as then withstand
   To yield the tribute of a sigh ?

Who quits even Yarra's winding shore,
   Where social charms yet scant'ly spring,
May call his fancy's view before
   Some joy to which his soul would cling.

Some friend in trying hour made dear,
   Some form towards which affection bends,
Some mate by kindred drawn more near,
   To the farewell deep sadness lends.

And ah ! to think mayhap we part
   To meet no more on earthly scene !
For rudest dangers frequent start
   Australia's shores and Thames between.

Cape Horn's frozen bulwark looms
   To stay our course 'mid stormy seas;
The icebergs gleam like fairy homes,
   As fair and fatal oft as these.

The Tropic zones we needs must brave,
   Where burning skies display their wrath,
And even Britain's hoped-for wave
   Presents a peril-compassed path.

In thoughts like these see the lesson lie—
   Our proven friends to cherish so,
That though we bid our last good-bye,
   Bright flowers of thought our memories strow.

SONG OF THE POLYNESIAN MAIDEN.

WHERE the sun dwells when flowers are veiling their
    bloom,
  They say there's a land with all beauty endowed,
Where mortals through pathways of pleasure e'er
    roam,
  Where life is all sunshine, undimmed by a cloud.
But I heed not their fables; they're idle and vain;
  Each clime has its seasons of tempest and calm,
And so Kallan is true, come gladness, come pain,
  The home I love best is the shade of the palm.

Though my robes be uncostly, my trinkets mere
    toys,
  Though my playmates be artless, my wooers un-
    taught,
Though the forest's the hall of our light festive joys,
  And each art that we know be with simpleness
    fraught;

4

Yet still am I queen of the loveliest land,
　　Where sisters and brothers I truly may call ;
Still fairest I'm deemed of the maids of my band ;
　　And, oh ! the bright concourse are bosom friends
　　　　all.

They say that this land is a land full of bliss,
　　Where men never sigh, or maids never weep,
Where sorrow's as light as the evening wind's kiss,
　　And pleasure, like ocean, as boundless and deep.
Though scant is my knowledge, those tales much I
　　　　doubt,
　　For sadness is ever twin sister to mirth ;
For though wisdom may smile and insolence flout,
　　My life shall decline 'mid the scenes of my birth.

A STUDENT'S ADDRESS TO LOVE.

I SOUGHT thee not, O Love! wherefore
   Torment me with advances rude ?
I've shunned thee as a dangerous power,
   And Pallas only have I sued.

Not but I know thy witching spell,
   The richest gift to mortals known ;
But soon I learned to know too well,
   Oft where thou art, there peace has flown

Nor must the toiler, who would fight
   Through strife and care his rugged way
Aspire to e'en thy blandest light,
   For such burns not thy genial ray.

Thus, Love, I tried to close my breast
   To all the whisperings of thy tongue.
Or, forced at length by thy behest,
   Woo'd Fancy's pictured scenes among.

Then Romeo's tale I sometimes told,
　　And gentle Hinda oft have sought,
But most with hapless Petrarch rolled
　　The strain that aids the wooer naught.

Not satisfied, you still pursue,
　　You haunt my pathways and my home;
Then if you must this soul subdue,
　　First yield this prayer wherewith I come :—

Grant that the maid who leads my heart
　　May all thy richest gifts enjoy ;
Nathless my vows no joy impart,
　　May Chloris' bliss meet no alloy.

Grant that the aged may blessings shower ;
　　Grant that the young may guard from ill ;
While maidens, curbed fell envy's power,
　　May own her charms the brightest still.

Grant her amid the good to shine ;
　　Grant her each earthly bliss to share ;
And make, O Love ! for thou'rt divine—
　　Oh ! make her Heaven's darling care !

TO * * * *

WHEN from the moulding hand complete
Man sprung to being, soul and mind,
With varying qualities replete,
With passions fierce or instinct kind.

Each impulse then to him was given,
All motives then did springing grow,
To shape his course or rough or even.
To guide his steps or high or low.

First in the garden of the soul
Ambition, soaring bird, took wing ;
Hers was a flight to mock control,
And past all curbing bounds to spring.

Next love of fame a home here found—
On high she looked with steady gaze ;
Her pride to make a world resound,
And win, for aye, unrivalled praise.

The patriot flame did next relume,
  With heavenliest light, the dreary void ;
By this is nerved the soul to doom,
  For thee the good and brave have died.

And love of wealth, and love of lore,
  And various promptings striving still—
Thoughts, feelings, instincts, wondrous store,
  Disturbed the breast or swayed the will.

Then pitying Mercy saw the storm
  That raged untamed man's breast within,
And bounteous sent a radiant form
  To calm the wild tumultuous din.

'Rayed in all loveliness and grace
  An angel did this comer prove;
Her blithesome form, her lightsome face,
  And smile benign proclaimed her Love.

Thus, thus dear * * * *, every thought
  Alternate sways my fancy free ;
But still returning care o'erwrought
  That fancy clings, dear girl, to thee.

A FRAGMENT.*

THE Roman's force in war and warlike arts,
The Grecian's genius and heroic parts,
The Egyptian's learned skill, the Persian's power,
The Macedonian's fire, the Frank's brief hour—
All these are themes that in the historic page
Shall live transcendent to the latest age.
But even now a story forms, whose pride
Above these other themes shall one day ride ;
Repressed each fault that in the warring jars,
His rage forgotten, and his wanton wars,
The Briton's fame in after years shall light
A glory 'mid these beams more fair, more bright.

---

* These verses were written in a small county town, nearly 200 miles distant from the metropolis, and were suggested by the wondrous evidences of the progress of civilization which were everywhere visible—a progress the more striking when viewed in relation to the apparently insuperable obstacles which had been overcome in carrying civilization so far into the interior of a rugged and inhospitable country.—Jan. 1855.

Not how he led his legions far and wide,
Subduing nations to his vaulting pride;
Not how he made of war a game, or framed
Huge, lifeless piles, unstoried as unnamed;
Not these the deeds his sounding name shall spread:
Far nobler works the Islander has sped.

How conquering ocean and subduing space,
The earth he traversed with a steady pace;
How unallured by love of golden ores,
He pitched his peaceful camp on doubtful shores;
How by no dangers checked or turned aside,
He pierced the forest, climbed the mountain side;
How leading commerce in the wake of toil,
He built up cities and subdued the soil;
While all the chaster arts successive came,
To gild and beautify the mighty frame;
How carrying out the great behest he ran
From pole to pole, the harbinger of man.
Such deeds relating—shall the historian say,
' 'Twas thus the Briton held his glorious way "

A LOVER'S PICTURE.

My love is young, and mild, and fair
As morning soft, as light as air,
When o'er the fragrance-teeming mead
The zephyr's balms their influence shed.
    The blue and beauty of her eyes
        I dare not, cannot tell,
    Their charm unmatched my tale belies,
        Oh, sweet their lustre's spell !

My love is loving, artless, true ;
Her words are scant, her glances few ;
Like fairy music on the sense
Those glances' thrilling influence ;
    And fair as budding lily's glow,
        Just opening to the light,
    Her spotless skin, surpassing snow,
        Transparent, lustrous, white.

My love is frank, good-natured, kind :
Not scornful, proud, or small of mind ;
Her tones are music to the poor,
And young men list but to adore.
   But ah ! 'tis heaven to think upon,
     Though kind and sweet to all,
   Save on my charmed ear alone
     Her words of love ne'er fall.

LINES, ON THE SAD FATE OF A YOUNG GIRL.*

FROM the water's dread embraces
Gently lift that tender form ;
Cold that heart, its tenant lifeless,
Once so fair, so pure, so warm.

Ah ! how altered—mark those features,
Beauty's home, joy's biding-place ;
See those lines, pale, cold, and rigid,
Stamped by death's abiding trace.

---

* A beautiful girl, named Kearney, who was attached to a military officer, followed the regiment to Dublin, in the latter end of 1851. Some time after her arrival in the city, having a quarrel with her lover, she threw herself into the canal, where her lifeless body was found. The allusion to the girl's country in the lines will be understood when it is mentioned, that, at the period of the occurrence, Ireland had scarcely recovered from the effects of the famine of 1848, and which, even in a land for centuries subject to frequently recurring evils, has not been surpassed in its horrifying details.—*Author's Note*, May, 1852.

Mark those tresses, erst so golden,
    Sadly weeping plenteous tears ;
Mark that cheek, the rose's rival,
    Like the shroud the hue it bears.

See those lips, which shamed the ruby,
    Fled the witching smile they bore ;
And those eyes, now fixed and fireless,
    Gone the enchanting light they wore.

Mark that brow, by bounteous nature
    Stamped with dignity untold—
Once surpassing marble's whiteness,
    Now 'tis more than marble cold.

Alas ! forsaken, lifeless, lonely,
    Strangers all around thee press ;
Tearless eyes are gazing on thee,
    Will no one mourn ? none redress ?

Far from childhood's haunts and kindred,
    None are near to mourn thy doom ;
Distant all, no clust'ring maidens,
    Loved in life, dispel death's gloom.

Like thy country's has thy fate been;
Gone love's sunshine, thou hast died,
'Reft of all who bravely loved her,
Long in death's shade has she sighed.

Yet one hope abides unfading,
Thou wilt rise in radiance bright;
And thy land, from sorrow springing,
Yet may glow in Freedom's light.

TO CHLORIS.

WITTY Chloris! arch young Chloris!
   Sweetest maid of Sydney town,
I perceive she grows a woman,
   And can take admirers down.

Yet I knew her when ten summers
   Scarce had breathed on her cheek—
But even then she was a lady
   Mixed of quizzical and meek.

Yes, her air was very queenly,
   As amid "those babes," she stood;
And her face was very solemn,
   Wearing its inquiring mood.

Rarely now she lights our pathways,
   True, the lads did gaze too hard;
But the treasure hide not, Chloris,
   Once was seen in thy regard.

Strong 's the preacher's word, when mildness
  Mingles with his meet reproof;
Strong 's the mother's look of sadness,
  For an erring child's behoof;

Strong 's the whisper heard within us,
  When the heart is good and sound;
But in Chloris' lovely features
  Better teaching far is found.

Yes, where grace and beauty mingle,
  There is virtue's surest friend;
I, for all that teaches goodness,
  To that face the world commend.

Triumph in your charms subduing,
  For your praise is spoken still;
But *I* sing not Chloris scornful,
  Chloris fair I ever will.

TO ❧ ❧ ❧ ❧ ❧ ❧

THOSE radiant eyes of brightest glow,
 Those flowing locks, with gold-light vieing;
Those blooms, like flowers 'mid winter's snow,
 Have long to me been cause of sighing.

Long felt I, maid, the pains that come
 From loving with a love unspoken;
As streams more deep will aye become
 Till bounds impeding them are broken.

In vain each devious art I try
 From thoughts of thee to gain diversion;
In vain I wander, vain I fly,
 My steadfast heart rejects desertion.

For everywhere that form still seems
 'Mid brightest scenes a sadness making;
For ever present in my dreams—
 For ever present in my waking.

Thus bound to love, I'll dare to woo ;

   Thus doomed thy slave, I crave thy kindness ;

Thus charmed, enthralled, dear girl, by you,

   I cried to thy—accustomed mildness.

IMPROMPTU.

WRITTEN AFTER A PERUSAL OF WASHINGTON IRVING'S
"LIFE OF COLUMBUS."

WHO war's unyielding work successful speed,
In victor's laurels still acquire their meed ;
A just reward, by fame, is ever found
For wit, for eloquence, and lore profound ;
While praise to statesmen due unceasing rings,
And patriots still are honoured more than kings.
But yet nor high renown nor splendid name
Can match, Great Sailor ! thy extended fame ;
For not on cities swept with wasting hand,
Nor one state ruined that the next may stand,
On certain evil, nor on doubtful good
Subsists thy greatness. justly understood.

'Mid best achievements e'er must stand sublime,
Secure of fate—still gathering praise from time,
That effort which, strong, steadfast, and alone,
To man bequeathed a world—a refuge—home.

INSCRIBED IN A BOOK PRESENTED TO A YOUNG AUSTRALIAN LADY.

BRIGHT as the skies which span thy land
  May flow, sweet maid, thy life's full measure;
And smiling Joy, with lavish hand
  E'er strew thy path with fadeless pleasure.

FOUNDING OF NEW SOUTH WALES, A.D. 1788.

UPRAISE your standard! Never thro' the days
  In nations' annals consecrate did rise
  A beacon yielding to the straining eyes,
Of future-seeing men, more hopeful rays.
Let war-notes rise in loud but gladsome swell,
  For never since the Orphean notes had birth,
  Did music herald to the tribes of earth
More glorious advent than your cymbals tell.
And as the signs that marked her nascent hours,
  So be the virtues of Australia's youth —
  A trumpet voice to speak the words of truth,
A lion's force to brunt war's sternest powers;
  While for the hour of peace her harp shall hold,
  These notes that flow but for the fair and bold.

OPENING OF THE FIRST PARLIAMENT, A.D. 1856.

WELL it befits that in the pageant show
    Matron, and bride, and maid, should hold chief
      place,
    Giving to gravest rites a livelier grace,
Filling the senate-hall with beauty's glow!
Men may found states, win conquests, freedom
      prize,
    But in the lapse of time, 'mid passion's rage,
    This truth we glean in each historic page:
Woman most bids a nation's virtues rise.
Old Rome's wise founder from the rabble crew,
    Received the fathers of the nascent State,
    But when his rugged legions he would mate,
From Honour's daughters he the mothers drew,
    And well Maturia, Clælia, Lucrece, tell
    Where greatness is, there woman's virtues dwell.

TO THE RIVER HAWKESBURY.

MAJESTIC flood, that glid'st 'mid shading trees,
  Seeking, like rarest good, a course unseen,
  How rich a lesson may the muser glean
From out thy heaven-writ page!   In thee he sees
A pilgrim that for ages held thy way,
  Blessing the land, when none did mark thy wave
  Save tribes unwitting of the good ye gave,
Waiting with patience the all-welcome day,
When happy homes should line thy bounteous banks,
  And maids, like Mary Anne, should bide
  Amid thy vales, and in thy sunny tide,
Mirror their graceful forms.   Thus yielding thanks
  For ev'ry fleeting joy, the true hearts know
  No change, let sadness come or fortune's favours
    flow.

TO THE HON. ROGER THERRY.

AUTHORITY is hurtful to the bloom
  Of all th' adornments that are seen to throw
  Around the paths of life their welcome glow.
No flower or balmy shrub dispels the gloom
That marks the high-set cliff; but round the base,
  Sometimes we see wild blossoms thickly strewn,
  Nursed by the sheltered warmth the rock has
    thrown.
Thus, Therry, did thy function but increase
Thy will and influence in the charming task
  To embellish life. The ermine, while it clad
  The judge, the accomplished man could never
    shade;
The jurist's gown the scholar could not mask ;
  The wealth of eloquence the wig replaced,
  While all the social virtues still thy presence graced

TO C. G. DUFFY.

Not simply, Duffy, for thy kindly heart,
  Thy boundless love for all thy kith and kin—
  The Irish people—dost thou greatly win
Our best esteem.   Nor for that higher part
Of mind in thee, so good, so large, so strong—
  The poet's genius and the poet's skill,
  With war, philosophy, and love to fill
The finished poem and the flowing song;
Though deemed good merits these, a higher yet
  Begets thy fame.   In thee we most behold
  One more of those, with dauntless soul and bold
Who 'twixt their nation and the wronger set
  The firm breast and brow—from Brian down
  To him the Chief of Peace whose name bespeaks
    renown.

O'DONNELL.

UNMEASURED plaudits greet thy name, good chief!
   Where'er old Erin's sons the sound shall hear,
   Where'er the scoffer's taunt—the doubter's fear—
Would damp the order of the fixed belief
That nations fall to rise. For holding still
   The tenor of thy sire's unswerving course—
   The widened current forceful as the source—
Dost thou not show how great the strength of will
When honour and the patriot's fires remain?
   Best vindicator of an exiled line!
   For thee two lands, not last of Europe, twine
The laurelled crown. Thy gifts to Spain—
   Strength, freedom, order, and a worthier sway;
   And Ireland owes—the reflex of thy honour's ray!

TO A JEWISH GIRL WHOM THE WRITER SAW AT AN ASSEMBLY.

In every feature of that glowing face,
  Where all the maiden charms do harmonize,
  Where all those graces we as beauty prize
Are found combined, how well the eye may trace
What speaks thee one of Judith's, Esther's line!
  As fair that presence as was hers who slew
  The Assyrian lord who would her race subdue;
Nor is the light which fills those eyes of thine
Less radiant than the light of hers who led
  Ahasuerus' will enthralled, and shared his throne.
  Methought, while bright 'mid brightest maidens
    shone
That spell-diffusing form, full well was paid
  Thy people's faith in this we still may see,
  While 'mongst their virgin throng they number
    such as thee.

TO MIRZE.

I.

THEE, beauteous Mirze! and gentle as beautiful,
   If e'er the feature indexed forth the soul,
   Late when I saw where graces writ the roll
Of all our city's fairest, when to cull
Perplexed the eye of taste, and had defied
   But that thy form was there to fix its gaze;
   Methought how hard that e'er that witching maze
Of charms into the beauty-waning tide
Of age should float.   Ah me! that polished brow,
   Ah me! those lips that like a bursting rose,
   The teeth that rival snow-drops half enclose.
Ah me! those eyes that cheering radiance throw
   Like kindly stars that through the tempest peep,
   When ships lie hopeless in the troubled deep.

TO MIRZE

II.

No cheerless thoughts will ever there abide
  Where Mirze's smiles diffuse a bliss around,
  For dull-eyed care still flies with lightning bound
Where blooming youth and florid health reside.
Late when I mused—wherefore did nature try
  To make a work so perfect if decay
  A few brief summers hence assert its sway ?—
An answer came each drooping thought to free,
For thee, thus Fancy spoke, Age has no mask,
  For thee Death's armourer no bolt would bring
  And when to mar thy bloom toward thee they wing,
They must but feign to do their graceless task.
  Thus all those charms will pass into the skies,
  And well if angels then continue wise.

TO ——, WITH THE "LUSIAD" OF CAMOENS.

An oak for ages gathered strength, and spread
  Its shading foliage o'er the verdant lawn;
  An eagle, from high air, admiring drawn,
Down stooped, and from the tree's cloud-kissing head
A bramble, with ripe acorns laden, bore.
  Centuries rolled, and its best honours shorn,
  That tree fast fades. The acorns, far off borne,
Budding ascend on earth's remotest shore.
Thus Lusitania's fame, by Camoens sung—
  Each rich possession and fair province gone—
  Shall live, and springing soar. Still later on
Should Lusitania's self—that arm unstrung
  Which served a mighty soul—sink a dead state,
  Her story, by her bard diffused, shall rise elate.

EVENING.

IT is the hour of eve.   The orb of day
  Being gone, the lamps of night in mellow radiance
    come ;
  As when in some cathedral's gorgeous dome,
The evening hymn being done, the awful ray
That 'lumined the high altar's sacred space
  Departing, leaves the lesser lights to throw
  Throughout the sombre aisles a misty glow.
How in the compass of a day we trace
The picture of a life ?   The morn, like youth,
  With light, and calm, and promise filled ; the noon,
  Like later years, when passions rage, full soon
To drive the wise to balmy fonts of truth ;
  The eve like age, when, seeing all earth bleak,
  On high men look, their guiding lights to seek.

LIGHT IN THE SHADE.

Even in the olden time, when books were rare,
  And men from Nature chiefly had their lore,
  The world, if wanting letters, lacked not store
Of sagest teachings for the student's share.
Who that e'er wanders thro' some bloom-floored
    shaw,
  When length'ning shadows come across the
    scene—
Night's harbingers, that spread the sunny green
With eve's appropriate carpet—he may draw
A lesson from the woods.   There where the shade
  Falls deep, the glittering, gem-like host ascends
  In brightest file, whiles, where the day-star bends
His latest rays, the beauteous clusters fade,
  Think, then, when overhead life's storm-cloud
    lowers,
  It is the shadow that calls forth the flowers.

BAYARD'S ADDRESS TO CONSCIENCE.

How much they wrong thee, Conscience! who
    would paint
  Thy form in terrors clad and fell despair,
  With face that scowls, and voice that speaks of
    fear
Not such thou art, and falsely they attaint
Th' angelic order who nor scowl nor frown,
  Who thus depict thee. Ever have I found
  Thee one whom beauty's mildest charms surround.
When, firmness falt'ring, I have wilful grown,
Or honour seemed to lose, in pensive mood
  Like seraph coming, Conscience, thou didst speak
  Reproving not reproaching, and didst break
Each ling'ring cloud that lay 'twixt me and good
  With beams of sorrowing eyes. Repressing still
  Each lesser fault, the germs of greater dost thou
    kill.

APPEAL TO POETRY.

As one with am'rous breast, and prompt to glow
  'Neath ev'ry wave of beauty's magic spell
  Loves without hope of winning, yet loves well,
Such homage, Muse of Song! to thee I owe,
And as the wooer, tho' resigned the prize
  Of love requiting, still the haughty fair
  Urges with sigh, and burning word, and tear—
Courting her glance, seeking her radiant eyes.
Tempting all arts at love's behest revealed,
  To win approval, or reward evoke—
  A small white glove, a rose, a silky lock,
Or, richest gift! a kiss—thus do I yield
  Thee warmest service, Muse!   Hopeless to gain
  Thy worthier bays, grant me some lesser wreaths
    t' obtain!

TO A LADY.

(SUGGESTED BY A SCENE AT A CHILDREN'S PARTY.)

THREE twinkling stars the star of eve around,
   When she, the evening star, lights all the sky;
   Three daisies lifting their bloom-heads hard by
A lily fair that soaring quits the ground :—
Such were the fancies that before me came,
   When late I saw thee 'mid the festive throng,
   Beside thy boy and girls, so fair and young—
Where all were young, and fair as words can name.
Nor was this ideal all. Are they not flowers
   Who know no guile, and deck each happy sphere
   Where their bright forms, e'er welcome, do
     appear?
Are they not stars, and more, who with the powers
   Divine that made the stars are close allied
   In soul, and yet above the stars will bide?

TO AN OLD PEN.

OLD quill that look'st so hacked, so grimed, so sere,
  Well teachest thou to practise lowliness!
  For all thy outward meanness, not the less
Might thy small nib work deeds—good, great, and
    rare—
Deeds that in all we prize would far outrun
  The mightiest work by wanton sword e'er wrought.
  The greatest victory e'er by life-blood bought,
Might pale before achievements thou hadst done.
In second Petrarch's hand how would'st thou write
  In e'er-enduring lines the tale of love;
  In second Shakspeare's hand how would'st thou
    move
Mankind, unmasked, before the spell-bound sight.
  With Goldsmith might'st thou every field explore
  Of wit, and thence deduce the choicest of her
    store.

MURMURINGS IN LONDON.

I.

LONE is my chamber, save that gently comes,
  To yield her solace sweet, my kindly muse ;
  Not so the adjacent street, where need and
    pleasure fuse
The city swarm.   There loud-buzzing roams
The busy crowd.   There thrifty housewives walk,
  To buy their Sabbath store.   Unmeetly joined
  There plods the female whom no joy refined
Shall ever bless ;   unholy heart, there stalk
The hoary ribald and the unthinking youth ;
  There haunts the beggar, and the robber crew
  There plan where they outrageous work shall do.
In such an hour and near such scenes of ruth
  I think of one whose life glides far, far hence,
  And pray my thoughts be worth her innocence.

MURMURINGS IN LONDON.

II.

FAIR is the temple towering to the skies,
  To teach the mighty city that above
  Lies the eternal land most worthy love ;
Fair each palatial home, where greatly rise
Virtues to guide a gazing nation's way ;
  Fair is the shrine, where monumental art
  Tells how the sage and hero played their part.
The park is fair, where gleam in long array
Fair Nature's sylvan banks. But when on these
  We gaze awhile, there comes a weariness,
  Time makes the grandest scenes to please us less.
One pleasure passes cities, mountains, seas :
  It is the joy the humblest mind may glean
  From the pure bosom and the soul serene.

POEMS WRITTEN IN YOUTH.

To — —

FAREWELL to thee, that bliss farewell,
  With thy fair form my fancy wove ;
No more to meads and flowers I tell
  In murmuring strains my ardent love.

Yet if thy image still could float
  Before my fancy's raptured sight
Apart from his, I still could dote
  On that dear form, so fair, so bright.

To thee I ne'er have breath'd my soul;
  My passion ne'er to thee could tell ;
So strong the tie, such firm control
  Had bound me in thy beauty's spell.

By looks alone our hearts communed,
   Oh! when did lips such language know?
By these I read a heart attuned
   To mine, beneath thy bosom's snow.

Yet can't I bear that racking thought
   That bosom by another pressed—
With anguish wild the image fraught,
   By thy embrace another blessed

Farewell to thee! that bliss farewell,
   With thy fair form my fancy wove;
No more to meads and flowers I tell
   In murmuring tones my ardent love.

TO IRELAND.

THOUGH far from the land where Shannon's blue
    waters
'Mid daisy-clad valleys so mightily roll ;
Where balm-breathing meadows and bright bubbling
    streamlets
    Delight the rapt vision, enamour the soul ;
Yet, oh ! my loved Erin, dear land of my fathers !
    From my breast thy fond image shall never
    depart—
Still nearest, still dearest, in joy and in sorrow,
    Dear land of my childhood, dear land of my
    heart !

Though *still* with thy sorrows the breezes are laden,
    Though thy glory and freedom should *never*
    return,
Though the song of thy praise ne'er a hand should
    awaken,
    And no soldier to right thee in battle should
    burn ;

Unchanged and unchanging, whate'er shall betide
    thee,
  This fond heart shall love thee till its life-spark
    depart ;
And its last aspiration to heaven be for thee,
  Dear land of my childhood, dear land of my
    heart !

PHŒBUS TO DAPHNE.

TRANSLATED FROM BOOK I. OF OVID'S METAMORPHOSES.

DAPHNE ! await, dispel thy vain alarm :
Sweet nymph ! await, no foe designs thee harm ;
'Tis thus, with beating heart and rapid pace,
The lamb avoids the cruel wolf's embrace,
The deer the lion, the dove the bird of Jove ;
Thus flies each creature all who hostile prove ;
Of my pursuit the moving cause is love.
How wretched I at each retreating bound,
Lest Daphne tripping touch the unworthy ground ;
Or, I the cause, whilst flying, faint with fear,
Thy tender limbs the cruel thorns tear.
The way is rugged where thy footsteps lie,
Restrain thy speed, fair nymph, less wildly fly,
And my pursuit arrested by thy stay,
My name and rank thy questions shall repay.

No mountain swain, no care to brutes I lend;
No clownish swain, nor droves or herds I tend.
Thou knowest not, timid, whom thy footsteps shun,
Else hadst thou ceased to fear and ceased to run.
The Delphic shrine and Clarion altars groan
With gifts to me, their incense clouds my throne.
The Ægean Tenedos admits my sway;
My sceptre, too, the Lycian realms obey,
My sire, he who rules the gods' array.
At my behest the books of fate unroll;
Charmed by my touch the lyre inspires the soul;
My arrow's certain in its airy course;
But one more certain, and of deadlier force,
Has pierced with painful wound my hapless heart,
'Till now unmoved by Cupid's direful art.
The laws of physic owe to me their birth,
I'm called the healer through the extended earth;
In sweet and grateful herbs the charms that lie
To me alone 'tis given to descry.
Alas! that herbs to love no cure afford,
And arts that all do bless, bless not their lord.

FABLE I.

A COCK that hunger's pinch long knew,
Upon a neighbouring dunghill flew,
To seek wherewith his gnawings might
Be for the present set aright.
He scratched until his claws grew sore,
Nor even then his toil forbore,
Without one particle of seed
Upturning, to relieve his need.
Till, having lost his patience quite,
He was about to change his site,
When something beautiful to view
Came forth—it was a gay bijou—
A diamond from Peru's mines,
That had been prized in other times.
The hungry cock a moment stayed
To view the glittering prize, then said—
" This to a Jew or gaudy fair
Had been a treasure *sans* compare ;

To grace the finger, deck the brow
"Twould answer well enough, I trow ;
But, ah ! to me one grain of maize
Were worth a thousand jewels' blaze."

THE MORAL.

'Tis not in glittering wealth contentment lies,
But in each humble gift our longings prize.

FABLE II.

(VERSIFIED FROM THE FRENCH.)

A MERRY fox, in former times
(I owe a fable for my rhymes),
A stork invited, to partake
At his expense, of a beef-steak,
And make him merry at his hall,
Away 'mid forest dense and tall,
Where Reynard oft found good defence,
When pressed right hard for an offence :
As helping goose or pullet rich
Down from roost or up from ditch ;
Or, as the Scriptures doth propound,
Lifting a neighbour from the ground,
That near some highway he had met,
And deemed for house and home hard set.
Well, to our tale—his note polite
The stork did answer with a flight,

And bowed with all a courtier's grace,
When he and fox stood face to face.
The table spread, they lost no time
To sit them down, and 'gin to dine.
The cover off, two plates came forth,
Filled up with richest steaming broth.
Stork made a dive, but lo ! his beak
Upon the delf resounded creak ;
For well you know from shallow cup
A crane or stork can never sup.
Fox in his sleeve at this *faux pas*
Did laugh right hearty—stretched his paw,
And helped his friend to some more food,
Until his dish had near o'erflowed.
" Your appetite, sir, is it keen ? '
The rogue inquired, with cunning grin.
" Very, indeed, sir," biped replied
(With hunger, faith, he could have cried).
Again he tried to have a taste—
Again he only made a waste.
He tried his bill in every way,
But no receipt his pains would pay ;

Yet still he "hemmed," and coughed, and
    said :
" 'Twas splendid broth, and very well made."
" Tis middling," modestly replied
The host : " I hope you're satisfied."
" I've dined quite hearty, sir, thank you,
(While inwardly he cursed the stew).
He took his hat, and bade good day ;
Bowed to his host, and walked away ;
Betook him to a neighb'ring. brook
With rapid flight, and hungry look,
Then set to work, and here at last
He caught a fish to break his fast.

APPENDIX.

———◆———

EXTRACTS FROM MR. FLANAGAN'S SCRAP-BOOK.

THERE is nothing fills my heart with a more bitter sense of degradation and indignity than that my equals, those men to whom neither birth, nor fortune, nor education, nor, I humbly conceive, intellect, can give any claim to superiority over me, should come upon me with the air of patronage and protection. —*O'Connell.*

There was a period of similar importance in the history of England. Franklin—Benjamin Franklin—with more of talent than any of us could boast, but with an equally sincere desire of combining America with England and perpetuating the connexion—the virtuous Franklin proffered the dutiful submission of the hearts and hands of America to be devoted to the service of England. And what did he require? A mere act of justice. How was he received? With derision, contempt, and insult. England refused to be just; she laughed to scorn the force of America. She even boasted that by the night-watch of a single parish all the armed power of America could be put down. It was deemed safe to oppress, and therefore oppression was continued. The Americans forgot their feuds, banished their domestic dissensions, combined in patriotic determination, rushed to arms, and—oh! may heaven be thanked for it!—

prostrated the proud standard of England in the dust and discomfited her with all her chivalry.—*Sheridan.*

The marks of that awful catastrophe, which so nearly extinguished the human race, are every day becoming more and more visible as geological research proceeds. Thus, in the limestone caves at Wellington Valley, the remains of fossils and exuviæ, show that their depths were penetrated by the same searching element that poured into the caverns of Kirkdale and other places.—*Captain Sturt.*

The conflict in his country's cause has, in itself, no terror for the Irishman. The maturity of life has reached me in the struggle, but yet my step is firm, and my arm, too, is not unnerved ; so that I should not feel any personal deficiency to deter me from joining in the battle's roar in the cause of my country. But I am not without my perception of passing events and instigating causes. Yes, coming events do cast their shadows, and I behold many circumstances which enable me to anticipate the future history of Ireland. The rising generation is not as submissive as their fathers were. It may not be equally safe to treat them ill as it is to ill-treat us. The rising youth of Ireland appear to have their pulses beating with better blood, and I have remarked more than once that, while I myself was tranquil, the eye of youth, scarce reached beyond childhood, was glistening with indignation at the history of six centuries of misgovernment which this country has endured. This fiery youth, with hotter blood boiling in their veins, is accumulating fast around us. Whilst we of the old day live, we can and will restrain them ; but when the grave has closed upon those who have been nurtured in submission, and trained in the toils of patient entreaty and constitutional prayer—when we are removed—oh ! may England, for her own sake, and for the sake of humanity, above all, turn off the evils which even a successful struggle must inflict upon Ireland—may she learn to be wise in time, and to be just while she may be so with dignity and pride. May she never force Ireland to imitate America.—*O'Connell.*

According to principles of computation which appear to be extremely moderate, the quantity of gold and silver that has been regularly entered in the ports of Spain is equal in value to four millions sterling annually, reckoning from the year 1492, in which America was discovered, to the present time. This in 283 years amounts to £1,132,000,000. Immense as this sum is, the Spanish writers contend that as much more ought to be added, in consideration of treasure which has been extracted from the mines and imported fradulently into Spain without paying duty to the king. By this account, Spain has drawn from the New World a supply of wealth amounting at least to 2,000,000,000 of pounds sterling.—*Robertson's History of America.*

M. H. GILL AND SON, PRINTERS, DUBLIN.